Little Women

Louisa M. Alcott

Adapted by
Mary Sebag-Montefiore

Illustrated by Christa Unzner

Edited by Lesley Sims
Designed by Louise Flutter
Reading consultant: Alison Kelly,
Roehampton University

First published in 2006 by Usborne Publishing Ltd.,
Usborne House, 83-85 Saffron Hill, London
EC1N 8RT, England.
www.usborne.com

Copyright © 2006 Usborne Publishing Ltd.

The name Usborne and the devices ♀ ⊕ are
Trade Marks of Usborne Publishing Ltd.

Printed in China. UE.
First published in America in 2007.

Contents

Chapter 1

A Christmas letter

"Christmas won't be Christmas without any presents," grumbled Jo March, lying on the rug.

"I hate being poor," sighed her sister, Meg, looking at her old dress.

"So do I," sniffed Amy, the youngest, who was gazing at passers-by. "And I don't think it's fair for some girls to have lots of pretty things and other girls nothing at all."

"At least we have Father and Mother and each other," said Beth.

"We don't have Father," Jo observed, moving to the sofa. "Not for a long time…"

"Perhaps never," each sister added silently to herself, thinking of their father far away at the war.

"Mother said we ought not to have presents this Christmas anyway," announced Meg. "She thinks it's wrong to spend money for fun when our men are suffering in the army."

At sixteen, and the eldest, Meg did her best to sound grown-up, but she didn't always succeed.

"Mother wouldn't want us to give up everything!" cried Jo. "And we each have a dollar.

We could spend that on ourselves. I'm going to buy a book."

"I'll buy drawing paper," decided Amy.

Beth began playing the old piano, skipping over the parts where the notes were missing. "A new piano's too expensive," she said quietly, "but I'd love more music."

"We deserve some fun," Jo added. "I suffer enough every day looking after Great Aunt March with her fussy old woman ways."

"It can't be as bad as my job, teaching those horrible children," Meg complained. "I hate having to work."

"My life's worse," Amy butted in. "All the girls at school laugh at me because of my patched clothes."

Beth put her mother's old slippers to warm by the fire. They were full of holes. "Let's not get anything for ourselves," she said. "Let's buy presents for Mother instead. She works so hard."

Jo beamed. "That's a much better idea. We'll go shopping tomorrow." And, seizing Beth, she danced around the room.

Meg and Amy clapped and cheered them on. As the pair collapsed in an exhausted heap, they heard the front door open. Mother was home.

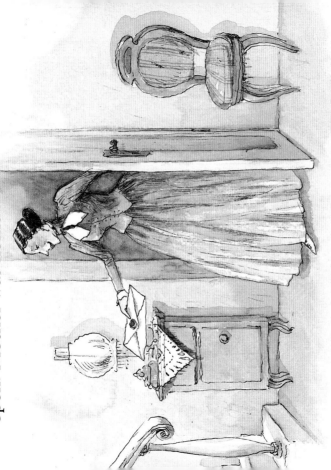

"I'm glad to find you so merry, girls," she smiled, coming in a few moments later. "I'm sorry I'm late. There was so much to do, sending food and clothes to our soldiers. But I have a treat – a letter from Father!"

Excitedly, they drew
near the fire. Their mother sat in the big
chair and Jo perched by her feet. She rested
her chin in her hand, ready to shield her
face and hide any tears that might fall.

Father's letter was cheerful and full of hope.

It seems a long time to wait before I see you again. Give the girls my love. I know they will be loving children, that they will work hard and conquer their faults, so that when I return I will be fonder and prouder than ever of my little women.

Chapter 2

The Laurence boy

After Christmas, everyone felt miserable. "Nothing nice ever happens to us," moaned Amy.

"That's not true," said Jo, coming into the room and tripping over Beth's cat. In her fall, she knocked ink onto Meg's hat, leaving a dark, spreading stain.

"Oh, it's ruined!" snapped Meg. "And I can't afford another. You are so clumsy, Jo! Beth, can't you keep that cat of yours under control?"

Jo shrugged her shoulders. "Was there ever such a cross family? But just wait. One day I'll be writing books and plays and be so rich that I can buy stacks of hats. Beth can have all the cats in the world and a new piano."

"Meg! Jo!" their mother called, coming in from the hall. "This will cheer you up — a party invitation for a New Year's Eve dance tomorrow."

"If only I had a silk dress and curled hair," sighed Meg.

"Your dress is fine," said Jo. "My party dress is scorched where I stood too near the fire *and* my gloves have lemonade all over them."

"You can't wear them then," said Meg firmly. "We'll each wear one of my good gloves and hold one of yours. And you must keep your back out of sight or sit."

"I think I'm going to hate this party," Jo muttered.

Amy stuck out her bottom lip.

"At least you're going. I wish I could."

"I'm glad I'm not," murmured Beth. "But I'm sure it'll be better than you think," she whispered to Jo.

The next evening, Jo helped Meg get ready, holding red-hot curling tongs to her hair. But soon she was thinking about her latest idea for a story... and a minute later she smelled burning.

To Meg's horror, a row of scorched curls fell onto her lap.

"Oh I can't do anything right!" said Jo, flinging down the tongs in disgust and rushing out of the room. Amy ran to console Meg.

"There," she said, fixing a velvet bow to Meg's hair. "Now it won't show."

As soon as they arrived at the party, Meg began dancing with her friends. Jo, who was terrified of showing Meg up, shot behind a curtain. To her surprise, she found a boy already there.

"You're Mr. Laurence's grandson," she blurted out. "I've seen you before. You live next door to us."

The boy nodded. "Hello," he said. "I'm Laurie. I'm hiding because I hardly know anyone here."

"You know me now," said Jo, with a grin. "I'm hiding because of my dress," she confessed, showing him the burn.

Laurie laughed. "Let's dance a polka down the passage where no one will see us," he suggested.

After their dance, Laurie went to get ice creams, which they devoured behind the curtain. By the time the party ended they were firm friends.

They were laughing in a corner when Meg limped over to them. "These wretched shoes!" she groaned. "I think I've sprained my ankle."

"Would you like a lift in my carriage?" Laurie offered.

"If it won't be too much trouble," said Meg. "Yes please!"

Mrs. March was still up when they arrived home, waiting to hear about the party. When she saw Meg, she fussed around her like a mother hen.

"We came back with Mr. Laurence's grandson," Jo said, as Mrs. March bandaged Meg's ankle.

"He's an orphan," their mother told them. "He's only just moved in with his grandfather. I must say he looks a nice young man – with excellent manners."

Meg hobbled to the stairs, thinking about the evening. "I felt like a fine young lady, dancing *and* coming home by carriage."

"I don't believe real fine young ladies could have enjoyed themselves more than us, in spite of our burned hair, scorched gowns and only one good glove each," declared Jo.

19

Chapter 3

Amy's crime

One morning, Meg came down to find Amy sobbing her heart out over the kitchen table.

"I'm dreadfully in debt," Amy wept.

"What do you mean?" asked Meg.

Amy sniffed. "I owe a dozen pickled limes at school. They're all the fashion. The girls keep buying them and I eat theirs and now I must pay them back, but I don't have any money."

"How much do you need?" said Meg, opening her purse.

"Oh thank you, Meg darling!" Amy cried, hugging her. "I'll buy them on the way to school." She didn't tell Meg that limes had been forbidden.

The news that Amy had limes soon spread. As the class began, a girl who disliked Amy shot up her hand. "Please sir, Amy March has limes in her desk!"

The teacher was furious. He made Amy throw the plump limes out of the window, one by one. Then he caned her hands in front of the entire class.

"You won't go back," their mother comforted Amy that night. "That school is full of spoiled, badly brought-up children. Still, it was your fault too. You did break the rules."

"I h-had t-to..." Amy couldn't stop crying. "It was so humiliating not having any pickled limes."

"I'll teach you at home instead," Jo offered later, picking up her hat as she spoke.

"Th-thank you," Amy gulped. "Where are you going, Jo?"

"To see a play with Laurie."

"Take me with you," begged Amy.

"No," said Jo firmly. "You're too young."

"Oh, please…" Amy wheedled.

"No."

"You'll be sorry, Jo March," Amy yelled at her.

"And I just offered to teach you!" Jo yelled back. "Spoiled brat," she added, slamming the door on her way out.

When Jo came back from the play, she started looking for her notebook. With panic in her voice, she asked if anyone had seen it. "Beth? Meg? Amy? Do you know where it is? The blue one, with all my stories in it?"

Everyone shook their heads, but Amy blushed a guilty red.

"Amy, you've got it!" cried Jo.

"No I haven't. I burned it."

"*Burned!*"

The whole family knew how precious the book was. Jo had worked on it for months, hoping some of the stories might even be good enough to print.

Jo shook Amy till her teeth chattered together, crying passionately, "You wicked girl! I can never write those stories again! I'll never forgive you!"

Beth flew to comfort Jo while Meg scolded Amy.

24

"I feel dreadful," Amy said at bedtime. "Please forgive me Jo. I'm very, very sorry."

"I'll never forgive you," Jo repeated. "It was an abominable thing to do."

Amy turned away. "Now I wish I hadn't said sorry," she snapped. "And I'm not. So there!"

The next morning, Jo was still furious about her notebook. Wanting to get out of the house, she asked Laurie to go skating with her.

Amy watched them leave from her bedroom window. "Bother!" she thought. "Jo promised to take me skating next time, but she's too cross. Well, I'll just go anyway!"

When Amy arrived, Jo and Laurie were already zig-zagging down the river.

"Keep to the side," Laurie called to Jo. "The ice is getting too thin in the middle." Amy, far behind, didn't hear.

Jo looked back and saw Amy coming after them. "She can take care of herself, mean pig," she thought, angrily.

Amy aimed straight for the middle but Jo skated on, with a strange feeling inside her. There was a sudden scream and the terrible sound of cracking ice. Jo spun around. Amy had vanished. Only her hood could be seen, bobbing in the water.

"Grab a branch!" Laurie shouted.

For a second, Jo stood frozen with terror, before she pulled herself together. She sped off and returned with a strong branch, to find Laurie lying on the ice, desperately clutching one of Amy's hands.

Jo thrust the far end of the branch into Amy's reach and helped to pull her, gasping and coughing, from the freezing water. Jo hugged Amy tight, swiftly taking off her dripping things and wrapping her warmly in her own dry clothes.

"Suppose she'd drowned!" Jo agonized, after she and their mother had tucked Amy into bed. "Sometimes I get so angry I lose control. I wish I didn't."

"I used to be just like you," Mrs. March confided. "Don't worry, Jo. I still get angry too, but I try not to show it. If you keep trying, you'll conquer your anger."

Her mother's quiet sympathy and understanding helped Jo more than any scolding could have done.

Chapter 4

Party girl

That summer, Meg was invited to stay with her friend, Sallie Moffat. "If only I didn't have to work..." she grumbled. Then, at the last minute, the children she looked after caught measles. "I can go after all!" Meg realized excitedly.

Her sisters helped her pack. "A whole week of fun!" Beth said, picking out hair ribbons for Meg to take.

Amy was green with envy. "Ooh, I wish I was going to a house party."

Jo began to fold Meg's skirts, looking like a windmill with her long arms. "What did Mother give you out of the treasure chest?" she wanted to know.

The treasure chest, made of sweet-smelling cedar wood, was where their mother kept her best things.

"A pretty fan, a blue sash and a pair of silk stockings," said Meg. "There was a length of violet silk, too, but there isn't time to have it made up into a dress, so I must be content with my old white cotton, I suppose." She sighed.

"Never mind, you always look lovely in white," Beth consoled her.

"I wish I hadn't smashed my coral bracelet. It would have suited you so," mourned Jo, who loved to lend her things – though they were usually too broken to be of much use.

"My white isn't low-necked and it doesn't rustle like a silk dress," Meg said crossly. "But it will have to do because there isn't anything else."

"You said the other day you'd be perfectly happy if you could only go to Sallie Moffat's," Beth reminded her. Meg gave a rueful laugh. "So I did. I suppose the more you have the more you want."

Meg was overawed by the Moffats' stylish and enormous house. She loved eating their extravagant meals, riding in their carriages and dressing herself up every day to go shopping and to concerts and on elegant picnics.

Sallie Moffat's pretty things filled her with envy, and home soon seemed bare and dull by comparison.

The house was full of Sallie's friends, all girls the same age, but not one of them earned a living like Meg. She began to copy their airs and graces and to feel ill-used and overworked.

The highlight of the week was the Spring Ball. The girls spent their time chatting about which dresses to wear.

"I have a new pink silk," Sallie said. "What are you wearing, Meg?"

"My old white," said Meg, blushing.

"Let's see," everyone begged.

As Meg displayed it there was a stunned silence. Meg felt them pity her poverty. Waves of bitterness swept over her as the others showed off their beautiful ball dresses, which billowed like clouds of gauzy butterflies.

"You can't wear the white. It's a day dress," Sallie said at last. "I know! We'll dress you up."

She called her French maid and between them they transformed Meg. They powdered her neck and arms, rubbed her with scent, rouged her cheeks, painted her lips and crimped her hair.

Then they laced her into a blue silk dress so tight Meg gasped for breath. The dress left her shoulders bare and the front was cut low. Finally, they decked her out like a Christmas tree, with bracelets, brooch, necklace and earrings. They even tucked a silver butterfly in her hair.

"Beautiful!" said Sallie.

But something had fled out of Meg.
Her simplicity and freshness had
disappeared and in their place was a
frilled fashion doll, no different from
any of the other girls.

Meg felt strange but excited as she
teetered downstairs to the ball in her
borrowed, high-heeled, blue silk shoes.

"Don't trip!" giggled Sallie.

To her delight, Meg found that the fashionable guests in the house party, who had ignored her in her shabby clothes, now swarmed to her like bees to honey. She loved being so popular and drank glass after glass of champagne.

She was flirting over her fan when she saw Laurie coming up to her.

"Meg! What have you done?"

Meg fluttered her eyelashes. "It's the new Meg! Don't you like her?"

"Not a bit," said Laurie gravely. "I don't like dressed-up girls. And what would Jo say if she saw you?"

Just then they heard people talking behind them.

"Mrs. March has laid her plans. She keeps trying to pair off one of her girls with the rich Laurence boy. Those Marches haven't a penny to their name. It would be a fine match for them.

Look at that girl. She knows how to play her cards."

Meg went pale under her rouged cheeks. "How dare they! It's not true."

"Don't listen, Meg. It's just silly gossip," Laurie whispered.

"Don't tell Mother and the girls about this," Meg begged Laurie. "I'd rather tell them myself."

"I won't," he promised. "But don't drink any more champagne," he added, in a brotherly way. "You'll have a splitting headache tomorrow."

Back at home, Meg told her mother everything. "I let them make a fool of me, and I flirted and behaved so badly. I just couldn't help myself – it's so nice to be praised and admired."

"Of course it is," said her mother, "but be careful your love of praise doesn't make you do silly things. Enjoy yourself, but be modest as well, Meg."

Blushing, Meg described the gossip she'd overheard. "Mother, do you have 'plans' for us?"

Mrs. March stroked her daughter's anxious face.

"Meg, my only plan is for you to marry for love. If you were happy, I wouldn't mind if you married a poor man or didn't ever marry."

"Sallie says a poor girl has no luck," Meg said.

"Sallie's wrong," said her mother firmly. "Be yourself, Meg, good and kind, and leave the rest to time."

Meg smiled at her mother. "Home may not be rich or splendid, but it's the best place in the world."

Chapter 5

Shocking news

When Laurie went on outings with the March girls, he often brought his tutor along. John Brooke was a thoughtful man, with friendly brown eyes and a gentle presence.

"Have you seen how Brooke looks at Meg?" Laurie asked Jo, one afternoon.

"Meg wouldn't dream of falling in love with him," snapped Jo. "She's tired of flirting and men. Come on, let's go to the post office. I want to see if there's a new story magazine out."

There was. Laurie and Jo brought it home. Jo flung herself down and read as if she were gobbling it up.

"Read it aloud," urged Meg. "We haven't heard a new story for ages."

"Brilliant!" was the general opinion when Jo finished.

"Who wrote it?" asked Amy.

With an odd mix of solemnity and excitement in her voice, Jo replied, "Your sister!"

Beth flung her arms around Jo. "Oh, you're so clever!"

"The magazine editor paid me for this one and he's asked me for more stories. I'll be able to help us all."

Mrs. March gazed at Jo fondly. "Your father would be so proud," she said.

A sharp ring at the door interrupted them. It was a telegraph boy bearing a telegram with the stark instruction:

44

To: Mrs. March.

Your husband is very ill.
Come at once.

Dr. Hale.
Washington Hospital.

Instantly, the whole world seemed to change, as the happy atmosphere collapsed around them. Mrs. March rose shakily to start packing. Laurie and Jo rushed from the house. Beth hugged her cat tightly while Amy simply stood still as a statue.

Laurie returned with John Brooke.

"Would your mother like me to escort her?" he asked Meg. "It's a difficult journey, and the war makes it even harder for women to travel alone."

Meg was full of gratitude. "That's so kind, John."

"Grandfather sent these to help the invalid," said Laurie, squeezing some bottles of brandy into their mother's luggage, along with a warm dressing gown, bandages and a blanket.

Jo raced in excitedly, her bonnet tied tightly under her chin, and handed a purse full of money to her mother. "Aunt March sent this. She said Father was stupid to go to war when he was so old, she knew no good would come of it, and she hoped that you'd take her advice next time."

Mrs. March tightened her lips, and Jo guessed that she was trying to keep her temper. But her mother only said, "Take off your bonnet, Jo."

Jo pulled it off and a cry rose from her family. Her beautiful long chestnut hair had been cut as short as a boy's.

"What have you done?" gasped Amy.

"I sold it," Jo said proudly. "I saw tails of hair for sale in a barber's window, so I asked him to cut mine off to get more money for Father."

Mrs. March was overwhelmed. "Oh, Jo. You shouldn't have."

"Nonsense. It will do my brains good to have that mop taken off. Besides, it'll be boyish and easy to keep tidy."

Amy fingered her own ringlets. "How could you?" she asked.

"She doesn't look like Jo any more, but I love her for it," Beth said softly.

Chapter 6

Beth

Mrs. March left for Washington at once. A week later, they heard from Mr. Brooke that Father was recovering. The news made everyone feel happier. Meg and Jo worked hard at their jobs, Beth and Amy cleaned the house and they shared the cooking.

But, one by one, they slipped back into their old ways. Meg spent hours reading John Brooke's letters. Jo curled up with her writing and Amy went back to sketching.

Only Beth faithfully carried out their mother's duties, taking food to families in the poorer part of town. One afternoon, she was drenched in a downpour of icy winter sleet. When she got home, the fire was out and she couldn't get warm.

A few days later, Beth started shivering as though she'd never stop. At the same time, she felt boiling hot. Jo found her looking in the medicine cupboard.

"I don't feel well," Beth muttered, going to press her burning head against the cold window pane.

Jo felt Beth's forehead and was horrified. "Beth, you're feverish. We must get the doctor."

When the doctor came, he looked serious. "The child has scarlet fever," he announced and sent her straight to bed.

Beth grew worse and worse. Amy was sent to stay with Aunt March to keep her out of the way and Meg continued to work though both of them longed to be at home. Jo spent all her time nursing her sister.

A bitter wind raged and snow fell. It lay in drifts around the garden, as white as Beth's face. During the restless, anxious hours in Beth's room, Jo realized how much she loved her.

Beth's shyness meant she was the quietest of the sisters, but her kindness and gentleness made her all the more precious. All of them had ambitions except Beth. Meg wanted to marry, Jo was determined to be an author and Amy dreamed of being an artist. Beth just wanted to make people happy.

One afternoon, Laurie caught Jo having a private cry.

"I wish I didn't have a heart, it aches so," she sobbed.

Laurie's eyes were wet too as he comforted her. "We mustn't give up hope. That won't help Beth. I've sent a telegram to your mother," he added. "I think she should come home."

Their mother came as soon as she could, brightness and courage shining from her. That night Beth's fever broke. The doctor confirmed it. "She's still weak," he said, "but I think she'll pull through."

Chapter 7

Endings & beginnings

Like sunshine after a storm, several peaceful weeks followed. In Washington, Mr. March was getting stronger every day and Beth was soon well enough to come downstairs and lie on the study sofa.

Christmas Day dawned mild and sunny. Laurie ran in and out with presents and Jo made ridiculous speeches as she presented each one.

"I'm so full of happiness, that if only

Father were here I couldn't hold one more drop," sighed Beth.

"So am I," agreed Jo, gloating over one of her presents, a brand-new novel.

"And me," echoed Amy, looking at a delicate framed print from her mother.

"I know I am!" said Meg, admiring the silvery folds of her first silk dress – a gift from old Mr. Laurence.

Laurie looked so excited he could hardly contain himself. "Here's another present for the March family!" he cried.

And there stood a tall man, muffled up to the eyebrows, supported by Mr. Brooke. "Father!" the girls cried. In an instant, the house was in uproar. Mrs. March was half-laughing, half-crying, Jo almost fainted and Amy fell on her father's feet and hugged his boots.

When they had recovered themselves, Mr. March was settled in an easy chair, Beth on his lap, and Christmas dinner was served. The fat turkey was browned to perfection and the plum pudding melted in their mouths.

Old Mr. Laurence and Laurie joined them, along with John Brooke, who kept sneaking admiring glances at Meg. She blushed and smiled back. Jo spent most of the meal glowering at the unfortunate tutor, much to Laurie's amusement.

They ate and drank and talked and laughed. The day ended with Beth playing carols and everyone singing.

The following afternoon, Aunt March arrived to visit her nephew and surprised John Brooke and Meg talking quietly together. "Bless me, what's this?" she cried, looking from the pale young man to her blushing niece.

"This is Laurie's tutor and Father's friend," stammered Meg. John nodded shyly, and vanished into the study.

"He's not thinking of proposing I hope?" boomed the old lady.

"He's not nearly good enough for you."

"Why not?" Meg demanded.

Aunt March sniffed. "He's a poor wretch and probably after the money he thinks I'm leaving you in my will."

Meg was so indignant that her voice soared louder than Aunt March's. "John's not like that! He's good and kind, which matters more than riches."

In the study, John heard every word. His heart swelled with happiness. "Perhaps Meg will marry me even though I don't have any money," he thought.

"Highty tighty!" said Aunt March.

"You'll soon tire of love in a cottage."

"I don't mind being poor," Meg replied firmly. "John and I work hard. We'll earn our way and be proud of it."

As Aunt March stormed off in a huff, John raced from the study and took Meg in his arms. Not long after, Jo entered the drawing room to see her sister sitting on John's lap.

Meg jumped up but John smiled.

"Congratulate us, Jo. We're engaged."

Appalled at the thought of losing Meg, Jo raced upstairs and begged her parents to do something. But Mr. and Mrs. March were thrilled at the news and so were Amy and Beth. Even Laurie dashed around with an enormous bunch of flowers for them as soon as he heard.

"What a year this has been," said Mrs. March, "but it's ended well."

"Hmm," murmured Jo, not liking the thought of her family breaking up.

Laurie nudged her. "Cheer up," he said. "You'll always have me."

Jo grinned.

"Don't you wish we could see into the future?" Laurie asked.

"No," said Jo, looking at her family. "I might see something sad and I don't believe any of us could be happier than we are this very minute."

Louisa May Alcott

Louisa was born in Pennsylvania, USA on November 29, 1832. Like her character, Jo March, young Louisa was a tomboy. "No boy could be my friend till I had beaten him in a race," she claimed.

Louisa loved to write. In all, she published over 30 books and short stories, but is best remembered for *Little Women*. She based the story on her childhood, growing up with her three sisters, Anna, Elizabeth and May. The novel was an instant success.

As well as writing, Louisa spent time in Europe, served as a nurse in the American Civil War and campaigned for women's rights. She never married and died in 1888, aged 55.